GW00730576

Nightshades
Tales From The Numinous Realms

EILY NASH

Copyright © 2015 Eily Nash
EdenDene Books

ISBN-13: 978-1518834172

Cover Image created using Canva

DEDICATION

A compassionate man once shared special words with me, his integrity and wisdom considerably altered my perception and brought great personal healing. I would like to share his words with you.

"Your scars are a story in a book, designed to be on the page and stored, like a historical novel. That's where they belong. They can stay in the page, buried, folded shut and put in the library of lots of other things that you don't need to be read any more. Closed book. Done deal. You are where you want to be, living in the moment of the new book you are writing, writing it as you go and unbothered by the dusty library full of old stories that don't inspire your new chapter."

I am indebted and grateful to Stephen Hynes for his words and also for co-writing the last story in this book, 'Over The Sea To Skye,' a beautifully evocative ghost story.

CONTENTS

ACKNOWLEDGMENTS

With love and gratitude to my wonderful husband Gary and our babies Jennifer and Ryan for your patience and support as I "word weave" gossamer threads onto the loom of ideas to become the material for my books. Oh and thank you too, my little fur-baby and muse, Angel the Westie. I love you all to infinity and beyond..

1 ANGEL OF THE NORTH

The sun was low in the Western sky. Warm fingers of pink and gold gently caressed a sleepy sky. It wouldn't be long until it vanished in a blaze of glory behind the imposing steel sculpture of the 'Angel of the North'. Another day on Earth nearly done and the promise of a new dawn still a distant dream.

The woman sat on the grass beneath the Angel's outstretched wings, her gaze fixed on the far horizon yet her thoughts were lost in a place even further away. A place where she had once felt happy and safe. A stranger stood watching her, unobserved. She didn't see the him or the steady stream of people descending the path back to the road below, nor did she see the flashing blue lights of the emergency services weaving through the traffic on the dual carriageway of the busy A167. The light was fading fast and night would soon come riding in. As the shadows started to close around her, the stranger was very aware of two sinister figures, dressed in black, making their way against the tide of footsteps towards the woman. Resolve crossed the man's face and he approached her before they could reach her. He made sure that they were very aware of his Presence. The shadowy figures retreated back down the path to the road below.

"Hi, how are you?" he asked.

The woman, jolted out of her reverie, looked up. The stranger, dressed in a crisp white linen shirt and deep blue jeans, stood by her at a respectful distance. Instantly she knew she could trust him.

"I am in pain..." She answered, her voice barely a whisper. A tear rolled down her pale cheek.

He reached out and gently sweeping her long black hair out of her face, wiped it away. A flicker of gratitude in her midnight blue eyes showed she had welcomed the tender gesture.

"Cassie..." she held out a slender hand, he noted long sensitive fingers and a very restrictive gold band on her wedding finger. The purple bruising around her slim wrists and the faded green one on her cheek, cleverly hidden by her make-up, did not go unnoticed either, nor did the imprint of angry red finger marks on her slender neck.

"D.I North." His grip was electric, his smile dazzling.

"Detective Inspector? No Uniform? Your day off?"

"I prefer to work plain clothes, find it's much easier to assist those in need of the specialist help I provide."

"So do you have a first name?" he saw she was intrigued. He saw her tears had stopped. She didn't pull her hand away, although he was very aware the thought crossed her mind.

"Raphael," voice as warm as the rays of the setting sun.

"Are you from around here?" both his name and golden looks spoke of a faraway place.

"Yes and No." Cassie noted where he was economical with words he was generous with the heat emanating from his hands. Healing hands. The concern of a stranger was too much to bear and Cassie blinked away hot treacherous tears. If she allowed them to flow there would be a tidal wave and she was unsure she would be able to stop. Sliding her hand out from his grasp she wrapped her arms tightly around her slender frame. He noted she trembled slightly and not from the cold. She was fragile and indeed in pain, and not of her own making.

"So what has brought you to Gateshead, Raphael?"

"Work. You..." It took a moment for his words to register.

"Me?" Disbelief.

"You!" his smile was a warm benediction.

"D.I? Detective Inspector? What have you detected about me? Why would you even concern yourself about me? What Department do you work for?" She searched his enigmatic eyes for answers to her flow of questions and saw only compassion reflected back.

"I work in the Justice Department. Cassie you said you were in pain, I see your body has been battered and bruised and you are suffering a great deal of mental turmoil. I detect your pain is emotional. You have been hurt. You do not need to be ever again. Your heart is lost and lonely and you search for something you cannot find."

"Yes... I seem to have lost my way, Raphael. I feel like I have been abandoned, a stranger in a strange land and I just don't understand the protocols of this world. There is nothing but pain in this place. People hurt each other just because they can..." A sob rose in her throat. "Those who say they love you lie and cheat and beat. They harm where they could heal. I have had enough suffering and pain and my heart aches and not just for myself."

"Yet the heartache brings with it a great gift Cassie. It brings empathy for others. It brings the gift of healing and Divine Grace, the pathway home." He placed his hand on her bruised cheek, willing the pain in her Soul to leave. A simple act of kindness. Too much to bear, she peeled his hand away.

"I wish that were true Raphael. I am searching for home, I look at the stars at night, searching, longing. I know home isn't here and I so want to go home."

"Cassie home is not a place!"

"If it isn't a place then where do I find it?"

"It is the very essence of Love and it dwells within your own heart. When others hurt you and lie to you or cheat or beat you then the sin is on their soul, not yours. It is not a reflection of you - it is a reflection of them. Time on Earth is finite. When one human seeks to diminish or degrade another, in truth, they only diminish or degrade themselves. Be the best person you can and always be true to yourself. Every act of kindness, no matter how small, is important and is recorded, as is every act of unkindness, nothing is unseen. In the fullness of time and with the help of my 'Department' the scales of Justice are always balanced."

"If only that were true..."

"The power of Light is far stronger than the forces of darkness. Divine justice will take care of everything." He fixed her with his benevolent gaze, eyes deep with the wisdom of the ages.

"We know he hurt you, he never will again. It is over. The scales have been balanced."

"How?" confusion reigned in her face and voice and she started to shake violently and the tears came and fell like bitter rain.

Raphael reached out and drew Cassie to him into a strong, protective embrace, almost as if an Angel had wrapped her in the pure essence of unconditional love. Understanding permeated Cassie's consciousness and she unequivocally knew that Raphael spoke the Truth and she would never need to search in vain for home again, home was within her own heart and her heart was not a prisoner to another.

The rapidly approaching blue lights came to an abrupt standstill, whilst their continued flashing and wailing siren signalled 'emergency' on the road below. Cassie finally took note of what was happening. An open topped red Mercedes lay overturned on its side and the paramedics were attending to a young woman slumped unconscious on the dashboard of the passenger side, her long black hair hid her face. The driver's seat was empty.

"That's my husband Nathan's car! Where has he gone? What's happened? Who is that in my seat? How did I get all the way up here?" Confusion and fear tore across her face as her questions tumbled out into the chill of the evening air.

Down below two men dressed in black suits were putting something into the back of a black vehicle marked 'Private Ambulance.' One of them turned and fixed his stare on her and Raphael. Even at a distance she felt a wave of malevolent energy and shuddered. Raphael pulled her close to him. Like shadows in the night the foreboding men slipped into the van and it melted into the line of traffic. Cassie stared, realization slowly dawning.

"Those men, they have taken him!" she exclaimed pointing to the traffic, but there was no black vehicle to be seen. Puzzled she turned to Raphael for reassurance.

"There was an accident, Nathan had been drinking heavily. There was an empty vodka bottle on the rear seat. He was speeding and the car skidded out of control hitting the trees. But you know this. You wanted to break free of him and leave. You had sent urgent and fervent prayers to God to free you from the devil that was your husband. He beat you and forced you into that car against your will. Cassie, you were lost, trying to find your way home. I was assigned to help just you. Nathan is now beyond my assistance. The 'Watchers' have taken him to the place where he needs to go."

"How do you know these things? Who are the Watchers, where have they taken him and shouldn't you be down there with the other Police Officers?" Panic gripping.

"I'm not an Officer, but you are right, my work here is done and you need to join them on the road below before the light grows too bright and you are unable to go back. The Watchers do not come from the same place as I do, neither they nor Nathan can touch you now as they must return to the darkness, as decreed by Divine Justice."

"What darkness and light? Who are you?" As Cassie drowned in bewilderment and the weight of unanswered questions, a multi-faceted, beautiful and luminous light surrounded Raphael. Then the night closed in around her and she lost consciousness.

Somewhere in the distance the plaintive wail of an siren tore through the cool evening air, as an ambulance urgently wound its way down the Durham Road towards the Queen Elizabeth Hospital. A paramedic deftly held his casualty's hand offering reassurance, whilst discreetly reading her vital signs on his monitors.

"Incredibly lucky to be alive, her airbag deployed, his didn't. Astonishing in a car of that value and specification. A miracle. Heart rate 62 and blood pressure 110/70 so all good, nothing more serious than just a concussion and some nasty old bruising by the looks of it," his voice level and matter of fact as he filled the driver in as to their patient's status.

His partner deftly negotiated the road ahead. "You saw the state of the car, there had to have been an Angel by her side to walk away alive from that one. The husband wasn't so lucky, dead on impact. Should never have got behind the wheel in that state and a wonder he didn't kill her as well as himself otherwise she would have been going off in that Private Ambulance instead of with us!"

"This one is a definite case of Divine Intervention!" The sense of awe in the paramedic's voice was perceptible.

As the ambulance pulled into the emergency bay of the hospital, through a haze of returning consciousness, Cassie heard their words and sent a silent "thank you" from her heart to her own special Guardian Angel, D.I Raphael North.

The last rays of the setting sun held the darkening sky at bay. Glorious filaments of red and gold illuminated the majesty of the imposing steel structure that is the "Angel of the North". With his vast wings stretched out over the surrounding landscape, Raphael sent a silent blessing out through the ethers to all those seeking their way home...

2 CANDLENIGHT

Lady Leonora shivered with a quiet thrill of anticipation. For it is said that on All Hallows Eve the Souls of the dead walk among men. Her velvet clad feet kept quiet counsel as she glided across familiar flagstones. Walking the length of the hallowed halls she allowed her thoughts to dance ahead to her Chamber. In darkness she reached the spiral stone staircase. Each familiar and well-worn step taking her nearer to her heart's desire. A faint glow of candlelight pierced the shroud of night. As a moth to a flame she drew near...

Darkness shyly approached the Castle walls and the woman welcomed its soothing cloak, gratefully draping shades of night over her unquiet Soul. A chill as fine as the threads of a spider's web graced the night air. Silence hung heavy. Although dusk had fallen, ancient tombstones, cold and grey, were visible through mullioned windows. They proudly stood as silent sentinels in the graveyard below. The swish of a gossamer gown broke the silence as her wraithlike form moved through the all-pervading gloom.

Bid by flickering flames of fire she knelt before a small bronze statue, which graced an altar fashioned from black onyx. Taking a pinch of Rosemary from a velvet pouch she sprinkled the dried herb into the flames. And waited. As the flame grew higher she whispered an incantation to the Immortal Ones. Nyx, goddess of the night and her celestial son, Morus, quintessence of impending doom. With arcane words she sought their intercession in her quest. Momentarily her chamber was cast into deep shadow. The gods had heard. It had begun.

Entranced, Leonora watched a story unfold in the dancing light. Bodies entwined in synergies of love and of lust, of passion and obsession, of hate and desire. The flame danced in abandon, gold and red and blue, until unseen fingers snuffed the candle out and a thin spiral of smoke faded into oblivion. The acrid smell of tallow hung heavy in the air. Tonight, the fate of mere mortals was in the hands of her gods and the story would have a different ending.

Taking a vial from her gown, Leonora drank droplets of the morning dew infused with a sprig of Wormwood, which had been purified over Sandalwood. And once more blood coursed through her veins and she blessed the life-giving potion for allowing her to walk between two Worlds. As Night came riding in she lit another candle. With occult words she chanted a spell to call her beloved husband Helios to her, for she was his Lady and he was her Lord and this castle their home. She conjured through the night, calling, calling. He had loved her deeply before the Stranger came and sang her Siren's song and so he would again. Helios would be with her once more. She willed it be so before the breaking of a new day took her ephemeral power, bestowed by the grace of the goddess of night, away.

"So Mote It be," whispered Leonora, a glimmer of hope dancing in her broken heart.

And as she waited by flickering candle light she remembered the love and the betrayal. She remembered she had held forgiveness in her heart. That was then...

In the midst of winter a stranger had arrived at the Castle Keep, penniless, alone and adrift in the World. She came seeking sanctuary. Leonora had embraced the lost and lonely stranger and welcomed her into the warmth and safety of the Castle, giving her food and sustenance, shelter and friendship and a place in her retinue as a favoured handmaiden. Sybilla with her long flaxen hair, eyes of innocent blue and comely face had a cold, black heart in which twin snakes of jealousy and hate lay coiled, waiting to strike at her benefactress. Helios fell for her charms and enchantment. Leonora had let the stranger into their home and her husband had let the stranger into his heart and his bed. He had lain with Sybilla, cruelly banishing his lawful Lady from his bedchamber. Leonora had pleaded with her Lord for the sake of their holy marriage vows to renounce his beguiling Mistress. She saw remorse and guilt in his eyes, she saw he was under enchantment and she saw that in time he would do as she bid. He would be hers once more.

Yet Leonora had a powerful foe, for Sybilla, having sought sanctuary within the castle walls desired to be more than a handmaiden. She coveted the title of

Chatelaine and wanted to possess both Helios and the keys to his castle. With deadly intent she plotted and schemed. Practised in the dark arts, she soon came between the Lord and his Lady. Having come so far, Sybilla was not willing to let it all slip away and give back the heart she had stolen from Lady Leonora. Something would have to be done to enable her to become Lady Sybilla...

And so it came to pass on a moonless night, with wicked whispers ringing in his ear, Lord Helios bade Lady Leonora join him in his bedchamber. With protestations of eternal love he reassured her that the small matter of his fidelity would be resolved once and for all.

With joy in her heart Leonora had heeded her beloved Lord's call. He had sent for her once more! With great care she dressed in a becoming gown of blue velvet trimmed with gold brocade. Her long raven black hair hung loose around her shoulders and placing a diadem of red Jasper and a veil of finest gossamer upon her innocent head, the bride prepared to go to her groom.

The Lord's bedchamber was candlelit with a thousand dancing flames. Her Lord bid his Lady come sip from a silver loving cup he had prepared for her. She lifted the goblet filled with deep blood red wine to her lips, and sipped. The wine tasted bitter. Helios smiled and vowed eternal love to his beloved wife.

The candles cast dancing shadows upon the rich damask wall hangings. Leonora shivered and asked if they were alone? Laughing, Helios reassured her there were no unseen foes hiding in the shadows. He urged her to drink another draught of wine. To please him, she drank deeply from the loving cup. The chamber began to spin wildly. One of the amorphous dancing shadows appeared to step out from the wall hanging and began moving menacingly towards her. Leonora gasped as the malevolent shadow took solid form.

Sybilla took Helios's outstretched hand. Fire raged in Leonora's throat as the goblet of malice, filled with the fruit of the vine and a rage of Monkshood, did it's deadly deed and she fell into Death's dark embrace.

By candlelight Lady Leonora's tears flowed as she remembered the vile transgression against her, his lawful Lady and wife, whilst waiting patiently in her chamber for her Lord to heed her tenebrous summons. Kneeling reverently, head bowed, before the black onyx altar she placed a simple offering of little purple flowers before a bronze statuette of her beloved goddess, Nyx. Her bouquet was formed from delicate Monkshood which she had gathered on this moonless night from her lonely tomb in the graveyard below. The poison within the gentle flower bells held no malice, only retribution. She watched in quiet satisfaction as the mellow candle light danced as it was reflected in a silver chalice filled with her own ruby red blood. Twin flames dancing in abandon, blue and red and gold. Her loving cup awaited him. He would come, he would drink her lifeblood just as he had taken it with his cup of tainted love and by the intercession of the gods of night, justice would be done and he would be hers.

Helios was doomed to meet his deadly fate that very night, fated to accompany his lawful Lady back beyond the veil where a silent grave awaited their quiet repose. Leonora would rest in peace with her Lord by her side through the passage of thirteen moon tides, until she once more walked in darkness to her chamber. Evil intent had stolen her husband, her title and her castle. A potent brew of retribution and revenge awaited Lady Sybilla. There would be no quiet repose within hallowed halls for her, only the gift of an unmarked grave far beyond these castle walls.

For it is said that on All Hallows Eve the Souls of the dead walk among men.

3 REQUIEM FOR LOVE

"Come to me and be my wife, I will love you all my life! My love is pure, my love is true, all I have, I share with you. Come Beloved, bide with me, in perfect trust and harmony!"

He once whispered those words of love to me. Our vows were sacred for all eternity. Alas, such promises my beloved could not keep. Oh how my wounded heart did bleed and weep.

You may well ask why did I not have eyes to see through his lies and mendacity? What was my crime or my sin? Why did He let the Stranger in? It was not my fault jealousy took hold! His words were callous, cruel and cold...

"I loved you once, that much is true, until her beauty stole my heart from you. She is comely! My lover is fair, with eyes of blue and flaxen hair. You grew ragged, grey and old. It is your fault my Love grew cold!"

My tears they fell like bitter rain. Illusions shattered, piercing pain. In the winter of my heart, I vowed from her he would part. I grabbed a knife and plunged it deep. Alas his life-blood ebbed and he fell to eternal sleep.

So now beneath the pure white snow, in the rich dark earth deep below, laid to rest two silver caskets filled with bones. By our silent grave my ghost atones.

Encased in ice my heart doth pine. In Death's embrace once more he would be mine. Eons pass, by my side he still lays his head. He does not stir, his body long cold and dead, his spirit left to be with her.

"Come to me and be my wife, I will love you all my life! My love is pure, my love is true, all I have, I share with you. Come Beloved, bide with me, in perfect trust and harmony!"

4 EDGE OF DARKNESS

As the Orchestra struck up the music and the dance floor of the Waldorf Astoria glittered into life, Johanna stood up. She reluctantly took the outstretched hand of her long time dancing partner, Old Nick. As he swept her elegantly into the diaphanous throng of chiffon and lace she stumbled over a fellow dancer's ill placed foot. Nick's vice like grip on her arm and steely glare ensured she would not cause him further embarrassment in front of his entourage of high rolling financiers, New York Socialites and Hollywood A-Listers. Nick was sure footed in all he did. Being seen as anything less than in control was not an option. Johanna flinched, his grip would leave an unsightly mark for all to see and she blinked away hot tears of anger and shame. It hadn't always been like this. They were so in step before...

Johanna Faust once thrilled at being in the company of rich and influential Nick Mephistopheles. He wasn't handsome and his age was indeterminate, but he had charisma and a dark charm. Nick's business practices were more than shady, but as long as she was on the receiving end of his largesse Johanna didn't give a damn what people said about him. There were rumours he was part of the underworld, they said there were other women but she didn't care. Johanna was a night girl. They said he ruled New York City and went for the jugular of anyone who opposed him. Was she afraid? No, it didn't seem to worry her, it gave her a rush. Greed fuelled the fires of her passion and lust for the man and his money. She didn't give a thought that there may be a heavy price to pay for his patronage when their first dance had begun twenty-four years ago.

"What kind of business are you in, Nick?" Johanna asked with an engaging smile.

"I'm a people person, a collector," his reply was enigmatic and further enquiries subdued by the string of exquisite black pearls he draped around her slender neck.

"How can I possibly repay your generosity, kind Sir?" She already knew she would do anything for him. The lavish Manhattan lifestyle was highly addictive for a girl from a Brooklyn brownstone.

"Oh, I guess body and soul should be payment enough, Miss Faust, yours and others I send you to collect!" There was a twinkle in his coal black eyes and she thought he had jested. Back then. Back when the dance had begun.

Nick was generous. Johanna only had to express a desire and it was hers for the taking, fabulous jewels, designer clothes, the Fifth Avenue apartment and the prestige of being on his arm.

Nick liked to work hard and party hard. He liked all eyes on him and he had a ruthless and vindictive streak with rivals in both the ballroom and the boardroom. Johanna was a huge asset to his dealings. Nick rewarded most handsomely when she performed. With a Siren's call her beauty brought victims to Nick's corporate lair. It was all a game to Johanna, well paid with a hint of danger. She liked that. The glitter and glamour was seductive and Johanna willingly checked in all morality and conscience as the years passed and she continued taking to the floor and dancing to Mr Mephistopheles tune.

Tonight there was unease in the air. Johanna was tiring of their 'Les Liaisons Dangereuses' and told him she wanted out. She told him she wanted more, she wanted love. Nick laughed in her face then grew possessive and wrapping his strong fingers around her neck he drew her close.

"Johanna, we have a contract. I own you, body and soul."

As she tried to pull away he kissed her hard on her ruby lips. There was none of the usual passion, just a stamp of ownership. She shuddered. The ballroom had become a prison and her dancing partner her gaoler. They had sealed the deal a long time ago. When you dance with the devil, there is no way out...

It was time for a new dancing partner. Nick would have to go. As the thought crossed her mind, she saw the Stranger and he saw her. And Nick saw him too. Savagely he grabbed her wrist, and snarled,

"Stay with me, Johanna. Better the devil you know..."

Johanna broke free and without looking back made her way across the empty dance floor. All eyes were on her but she saw no one only the charismatic stranger. He seemed to emit a numinous light. Music sublimely filled the ballroom and she moved inexorably into his arms.

"Do you want to dance?" she whispered seductively.

"Only, if you are willing to forsake Nick's protection and come with me to the end of time, Johanna." He brushed her face with beguiling lips which sent shivers down her spine and shuddering she realised his mouth was as cold as the grave.

"I will..." she paused looking back at Nick's table, both he and his entourage were nowhere to be seen.

As the stranger held out his hand, it dawned on her he knew her name but she did not know his. Just who was this beguilingly beautiful man? With prescience he smiled and answered the question swimming in her mind.

"Lucifer."

As she gasped, he swept her into his arms and onto the dance floor. The Orchestra struck up the music and the hypnotic strains of Ravel's Bolero filled the air. The Last dance would truly last forever as Johanna danced with the devil to the edge of darkness...

5 STAIRWAY TO HELL

The snow lay round about deep and thick and Ellis stood at the bedroom window watching the soft flakes falling, so perfect, so pure, so white. In the background the radio was playing a favourite song of hers about love, loss and betrayal. The vocalist's voice harsh against the plaintive notes of his melancholy mandolin. The lyrics rattled in her head, so familiar she could have penned them herself. And once again, she saw herself hurtling back in time and finding herself dancing with the devil on her own private stairway to hell. The husband, who had so fooled her when she first met him, with beguiling green eyes masking the savagery in his soul. Charm the camouflage hiding the demon that dwelt within him, content to remain hidden until she was shackled to him *'for better, for worse'*...

Only, no one told her there was no better...

She had heard there was a name for it. Post-traumatic stress...The flashbacks and vivid replay of events in full widescreen Technicolor, like a DVD inserted into your brain jammed on replay with no eject button. They were insidious invaders those memories, cunning and crafty, hiding in the dark recesses of your mind and ready to pounce when they caught you unawares. Then once they had you in their gleeful grip, drag you kicking and screaming down into the depths of deep despair. Down the jagged staircase into the hell of your own private screening room, where the walls were padded and no one heard you scream.

It might be a sight, a sound, a word, anything but once the association had been made there you were, spiralling into the unrelenting loop of the synaptic storm unleashed in your mind. Trapped, until you were left battered, bruised and bleeding. Shaken to the core of your very being.

A captive prisoner, watching it all unfold in your mind, with your body frozen in fear. Time after time it grimly ran its course and you a reluctant observer, eyes fixed on the private screening of your own personal horror movie, forced to experience it all, again and again.

With her psyche screaming in pain, Ellis felt her soul dis-associate as the furies rushed in and excoriated the flesh from her body. Carrion sacrificed on the rocks of life awaiting the purification of a sky burial once the raptors came and carried the putrefying flesh away. Release.

When it was over toxic tears came and like blessed rain washed all the filth and dirt away and the haunting strains of the melancholy mandolin hung in air.

I passed you on a stairway
Somewhere back in time,
I just had to make you mine!

You tried to take me your way
Up where the skies are blue,
I had other plans for you...

You wanted to go towards the light,
I dragged you down into the night
Through depths of dark despair.

Welcome home to the devil's lair.
I pushed and you fell
Down the stairway to hell...

6 CATS EYES

The lone horseman cut a shadowy figure, barely visible threading his way through Sherrards Wood. The trail was overgrown and difficult for both man and beast to negotiate, especially as the weather had a mind to be unkind and inclement this winter's eve. It was a night to be fireside with plates piled high with good food and fine wine served by comely wenches. He cursed vehemently as the cold rain began soaking through his opulent velvet cloak, the fur trim sticking uncomfortably to his skin. The north wind, having taken a dislike to the man, had a mind to torment him and screeched obscenities right back at him.

Unsettled by the strange shadows prowling through the trees and the howling wind Favian made haste. He violently dug sharp spurs into his horse, urging it to break from its steady canter into a gallop. Almost expecting to see a pack of baying hellhounds giving chase he glanced over his shoulder, unaware the path was narrowing ahead. The hoot of a barn owl startled his steed, and spooked, it lurched to the left into dense undergrowth. The move was unexpected and before the man could gain control of the reins angry brambles scratched and tore at his noble face. Favian shouted at the horse as he felt a hot trickle of blood coursing down his cheek, rivulets of red running over his lips. The taste of iron was bitter and he spat in distaste, wiping his mouth with the back of his gloved hand. Savagely he used his whip on the animal's flanks, blaming the innocent creature for his discomfort.

By the time Favian reached his destination he was in a foul mood. He would not have ventured out on such a night if it were not of such import. Dismounting, he tied Ned his uncomplaining old horse to an ancient chestnut tree. There was no thought to the creature's well being. It had been a long hard ride and food or water would have been welcome. There was none to be had. Instead the man reached deep inside his cavernous cloak searching for a comforting leather flagon filled with mead. Once he had seen to his needs and availed himself of a long draught of the sweet tasting and warming liquor he strode purposefully towards a dilapidated hovel. Standing forlornly within the forest clearing it was a far cry from the opulence within his father's castle walls. A spiral of thin grey smoke rose up into the damp night air, whatever comfort it brought was carried away on the howling wind. The crackling of broken twigs caused the hairs to rise on his neck. For a moment he hesitated. A sense of foreboding came over him and he felt uncharacteristically afraid. Drawing in his breath and a dagger from his side and with feral eyes searching for hidden foes, he was on high alert. The skinny black cat that rushed by him was a huge relief and aiming a misplaced kick at the cat he laughed as it turned, arched its back and hissed. Another deep swig of the mead strengthened his conviction and he followed the creature towards the hovel. The cat was sat outside a weather beaten wooden door staring directly at him. Its amber eyes were penetrating and he had the uncomfortable feeling the creature was boring into his mind. He shook himself, he was not a fanciful man, it was only a cat not some phantasmagorical creature of the night the villagers spoke of in hushed and fearful tones. Favian was strong, and if not for an accident of birth as the second son of a nobleman he would be on the brink of becoming the most powerful Lord of the Manor in these parts. The cat was in his way. Favian did not like anything or anyone to stand in the way of what he wanted. Without a second thought he unsheathed his dagger and took aim.

His face clouded darkly at the thought of what might have been if it were not for his weakling of a brother. With only a matter of days, if not hours, before the Lord of the Manor breathed his last it would all fall into his unworthy hands. Favian spat in disgust at the thought of Florian, his pathetic sibling whom he had left sobbing at their aged Father's deathbed inheriting everything. The heir should have been him. He was the man to own the castle and the lands far beyond its walls. He should be the one with men to command, swearing allegiance to no one but the King himself. He should be the one to marry Estella, the comely and virtuous maiden chosen for his brother's bride. The thoughts burnt as raging coals in the furnace of his mind. It should have been him! He deserved no less. Life was unfair! His were the eyes that saw her first, the French beauty with flaxen hair wound and bound around her proud head and dancing eyes of cobalt blue. He had shown his devotion to her on the jousting field. Yet she had spurned his ardent displays of valour in favour of his weak sibling. How could she prefer Florian's vapid utterings of courtly love, serenading her with the songs of the Troubadours, to his manly valour?

As his Father's second son arrangements had already been made for him to enter the church. His future mapped out for him, a future he did not want. It was not what he deserved. A future life as an Abbot was not to his taste, something had to be done and it had to be done now, before it was too late. The hovel before him held the solution. He had come this far and now there was no going back.

He seethed recalling the scene that had become etched in agonies of jealousy upon his mind, robbing him of sleep and peaceful repose. Florian and Estella locked in a tight embrace beneath the eastern tower, whilst he remained unseen listening from a window above.

'Ah Estella, my heart aches for Father and his plight. I fear the days to come. If there were another way I would keep my brother close, but I have seen the darkness growing in his jealous heart. He would see me join our Father in death's embrace and take you to his side!'

'Fear not, my beloved Florian, for I will be forever at your side, two hearts entwined as one. Favian has a cruel and vindictive streak. The powers that be would not allow for him to become the next Lord of this Manor. If ever two brothers were so different! One of you pure heart, the other with a heart as black as night. He would not rule with wise council and grace, as you will my love.'

'He does not want to enter the confines of the church, but Father and I decided he is far too brutal to take on the auspices of Knighthood.'

'Chivalry is not in his dark nature, Florian. The church may well prove safe haven for his eternal soul. Come my love, let us return to your Father's side. Eliza has brought me a potion of Meadowsweet and Wood Sorrell she prepared in the herborium to aid him in his hour of need.'

'You are indeed blessed to have her as your handmaiden for she comes to you with many talents born of an ancient lineage, my love. Those amber eyes of hers hold much knowledge.'

'Indeed Florian, for one so young she is well versed in the old ways, which are always useful in dangerous times such as these.'

Hand in hand they had walked back into the castle and to his Father's bedchamber.

With a sense of urgency Florian sought out Eliza...

The interior of the hovel was dark, lit by a single stumpy candle formed from tallow, and it took Favian a moment or two to acclimatize to the gloom. The tallow smelt acrid and unpleasant and he sniffed in distain. A creak drew his attention and he made out the shape of a crumpled old woman sat fireside upon a wooden stool. She was wrapped in a thick woollen shawl over a dirty black skirt. Her feet were bare and coated in the grime of the forest floor. The cat was nowhere to be seen, despite having evaded his dagger and run through the door which had creaked open seconds before Favian had made his unceremonious entrance. A sudden movement and the fire sprang into life casting a low glow. A blackened pot hung on a hook above the grate. Burning embers added much needed illumination to the pitifully poor interior. It was almost threadbare apart from a rocking chair and a trestle table laden with jars of potions and bunches of dried herbs and flowers. The old woman broke into an unexpectedly raucous cackle and the cavern of her mouth gawped open exposing a few rotten teeth within her wizened maw. Her face was lined and wrinkled by the ravages of time and strands of straggly white hair covered her eyes.

'What can I do for you good Sir Favian?' Her polite enquiry was laced with sarcasm.

'Eliza sent me,' he stated starkly, not questioning she knew who he was.

'Oh.' There was no surprise in the voice that answered.

'Eliza told me you practice the Arts.'

'What Arts would they be? What would an old woman such as myself know of Arts? I live a humble life, living of the land and grateful for the charity of those good of heart.'

'Pah! Don't play with me old woman,' he menacingly bent his large frame into her frail body. 'It is said by those superstitious villagers that you are an adept of the dark arts.'

'It would be very foolish to claim such powers. You know what villagers are like with their silly gossip about witchcraft and the like.' She left her words hanging coldly between them.

'Eliza is not given to gossip. That girl knows things!'

'Aye, she may well do so Sir Favian, but I dare say what she knows she shares only with those she trusts within your Father's walls and keeps her own counsel.'

'And she did too, until I beat it out of her!' he spat in frustration.

The old woman responded icily 'did you indeed? Was there any need for that? Eliza has been a true and loyal maidservant to the Lady Estella and your noble family. I hear you tried to make good use of both those fair ladies yourself. I hear your Father has made provisions for you to enter the Church.' Her voice was loaded with contempt.

Favian clenched his fists, face red with rage. He would have swung for the helpless old woman, but he needed her. His eyes grew cold and he resolved once he had what he had come for she would get what she rightly deserved for such insolence. They burnt witches and no one would doubt his testimony the old hag had put a spell on his brother causing him a quick and painful death. He smiled at the thought of all his plans coming to fruition. With his Father dying, his brother dead and the Manor all but his nothing would prevent him taking the lady Estella for his wife. And as for the comely Eliza, there would be no one to protect her and keep him from her bedchamber now. It would not be long until he got just what he rightly deserved.

'A man in my position gets what he deserves, and more, that is why I am here and you will help me get what is rightfully mine.' He crouched down low and grabbed the old woman's wrists in a vice like grip. 'Eliza said you practice the dark Arts. She said you were the only one who could give me what I deserve, and give it to me you will!'

'Unhand me and tell me what it is you want, I will not be able to practice the Arts you speak of with broken hands.'

'I want control of the Manor and all the land and villagers. The old Lord is on his deathbed and I should be his heir.'

'Does not his Lordship have a firstborn son, your brother? You are but a second son, the right of title will not pass to you.'

'Aye, what you say is true, but with less than a year between us my brother is everything I am not. He is weak and his support for King Stephen over the Empress Maude could loose us everything in these dangerous times. As Lord of the manor I will pledge allegiance to Maude and her cause. I will receive great riches and rewards for my loyalty!'

'There are many in these parts would call that treachery Sir. King Stephen is the rightful heir and his support is strong. You could loose everything, The King is not a forgiving man, so it is said. But how can I help with such matters?'

'You were the one taught Eliza the power of potions. I need such a potion. I need something to remove the obstacles in my path to my destiny. I need what I deserve and I need it now, tonight!'

'Then why did you not ask Eliza for such a potion?'

'She said her skills were in healing and removing those things that ail a body. I beat the truth out of her, she sent me here to get what I deserve from one practised in the old ways and the dark Arts. I am done conversing with you old woman; give me what I ask for. I will have what I rightfully deserve before day break.'

'Hmm. Indeed I shall use my Arts to give you what you deserve, Sir Favian. If it is your will and you so desire it, then confirm your intent and it shall be so, but I warn you once the spell has been cast to give you what you rightfully deserve there will be no going back. Death will occur and what has been engendered cannot be undone.'

'I do desire it.'

The old woman stood up and walked over to the trestle table. Carefully she rooted through the bottles and herbs. Selecting those she required she returned to the fire. There are indeed herbs that heal and there are also herbs that harm. Throwing sprigs of henbane onto the fire, she began chanting arcane words. The fire began to spit and growl as angry flames grew higher.

Favian stood before it lapping up the warmth, satisfied it had begun. The chanting grew more urgent and the flames intensified.

'Are you sure I should continue?' she asked.

'Do it!' he replied excitement of what would rightfully be his consuming him.

The old woman opened a vial of a foul smelling liquid and cast it onto the fire, her woollen cloak slipped to the floor. She did not look frail now. Her hair was no longer white, but a blanket of black cascading down her back. Through billowing smoke he could just about make out her shape as she stood tall and proud. As she added more herbs and resins, the smoke cleared. Favian saw her eyes for the first time. Luminous, deep amber eyes. Eliza's eyes. Shocked he blinked and she was gone. With a roar, flames of blue and gold chased red sparks up the chimney. Favian gave a gasp, it seemed as if the gates of hell were opening. Fire and brimstones spewed out into the room and began encircling him. In fear he cried for it to stop. A cackle filled the air. The only reply was a vicious hiss from the black cat as it stepped out of the cloak on the floor, fixed him with deep amber eyes and sauntered out of the door.

7 AN ANGEL CALLS

Midwinter. A fog began to descend over the grey London skyline. Dusk had stealthily crept in and stolen the remains of the day away. The elegant terrace of Victorian villas took on a ghostly air, cloaked in numinous mist. The warm orange glow of fires burning cheerfully in elegant parlours gave a reassurance that all was well within each dwelling. Smoke snaking from tall chimney pots into the chill air warned the creatures of the night to stay away.

One house stood apart from the camaraderie of its neighbours, no warmth or light was to be found within. As dusk gave way to night the fog began to lift. Gas lamps were extinguished and weary folk made their way gratefully to bed, giving thanks to the Lord for the day that had just been done and the morrow yet to come. The interior of number four was just as bleak as the façade. The winter's night seemed to penetrate through the outside walls into the very heart of the despondent house. Cold and eerily empty, apart from the first floor bedroom where two figures lay snuggled under a damask counterpane upon a huge mahogany bedstead, a dark island in a sea of grey shadows. Heavy brocade curtains, slightly drawn, dressed the large Victorian window. Although slightly closed they admitted a sliver of pale moonlight. Deftly cutting through ominous clouds scuttling across the sky and creeping into the gloom, illuminating the scene within the room. Furnished with heavy, dark mahogany furniture of a bygone age it was out of step with the world unfolding beyond melancholy walls.

A young child sat up on the huge bed, cornflower blue eyes wide open, scanning the gloom for an unknown yet threatening Presence. She drew the counterpane tightly around her small frame for security. Warily tucking the edges under her little heart shaped face, framed by a mass of tumbling golden ringlets, she looked almost fey. The rich cloth seemed to provide a degree of safety and comfort. The big bulky frame of her Father afforded a wall of protection as he lay sleeping heavily. His stentorian snores reverberating around the cavernous room offered reassurance, breaking the mounting terror of creeping silence. Huge, menacing shadows thrown up by arbitrary beams dancing through the darkness were too much to bear and a strangled sob escaped into the room. The Father stirred, and seeing his tiny daughter wide awake, urged her to snuggle down and sleep. As the capricious moonlight fell across the floorboards, it revealed a languid shape lying comatose. The flaccid form slumped with an empty brandy bottle clutched in a lifeless hand. A bottle of laudanum, also empty, lay close by. The little child was worried.

'No Papa!' She shook her head, her golden ringlets swaying, and eyes luminous and anxious, enquired tentatively 'Is Mama cold lying there on the floor? Should Mama get into bed too? Shall we cover Mama with her shawl to keep her warm?'

Thinly veiling his feelings of revulsion and contempt and voice laden with disgust, the tired man reassured her.

'Mama is fine, Violet, she has merely had another fit of the vapours. Mama is where she wants to be and we shall leave her there undisturbed. Go back to dreamland, my sweetkin.' Then he rolled over and went back to sleep.

The little girl burrowed under the covers, and snuggled into the soft counterpane. Mama was fine, Papa knew best and reassured she slept the rest of the night soothed by the deep sleep of the innocent. In her dreams she called for an Angel, an Angel of Love and Light, and the Angel hearing her call came.

The room was suddenly bathed in a luminous golden glow and the Angel stepped out of the light with her arms outstretched. She held a gossamer blanket, woven from the light of the stars in the heavens above, and gently she wrapped the child's Mother in love and light and tenderness. For the Angel knew the woman was bound by the demon of addiction. The demon hissed, 'She is mine!'

The Angel knew that barricaded into her own pain, it would take a lifetime to free the woman from her tormentor and captor. How long that life would be was written in the stars. The demon pushed the laudanum bottle across the floorboards. The woman stirred and through a haze of drugged drunkenness she reached for the bottle and taking it from him she drained the last dregs. In his clawed hand the demon held a fresh bottle. The woman lunged at him, eager to feed her addiction.

'It is yours, but not whilst you clutch at that useless thing!' he spat, pointing his gnarled claw at the blanket of light.

The blanket of Light felt good and through the haze of drugs and alcohol the woman knew she should keep a tight hold.

'Go away!' She cried, wrapping the blanket tightly around her body and peace soothed her unquiet soul. The demon left and the woman slept, fitfully. She was still a beloved child of God and deserving of love and forgiveness and understanding. The Angel prayed silently and bestowed a quiet benediction over the child and her lost Mother and also the man who had long forgotten the truth, as he slept in his warm bed whilst the woman he once loved and had lost her way lay on the cold floor.

A fragrant blend of frankincense and attar of roses filled the room. The rank smell of stale alcohol and the bitter pungency of the opiate that had pervaded the air now dissipated. The man did not smell the fragrant perfume purifying the space around him, his child and his wife. Nor did he see the celestial blanket of stars wrapped around her. He did not see the Angel of Light standing at the foot of the bed, waiting. The demon would return. The woman would fight. Without the help of the man her redemption would only come the other side of the veil. But he was unable to feel the Presence of God when an Angel calls...And so the Angel wept.

8 THE BOWER

Deep within the darkest heart of night
dance slender beams of soft Moon Light.

Brushing aside the despair cloaking the ancient ruins, La Luna's children playfully danced amid dank and gloomy walls all that remained of the glories of the past. With carefree abandon, darting moonbeams brought illumination to the derelict Eastern Tower, a silent Sentinel withstanding the ravages of time, proudly giving testament to the pride and glory of bygone years. Those who once lived and loved within the Castle's protective embrace are but jagged shards of memories, forever entombed within decrepit walls. Yet there remains a solitary voice from long ago compelled to whisper her sadness upon the wind. Trapped by her heart she cannot leave her lonely Bower within the Castle Tower.

By the light of the moon, at her lonely loom, sits Lady Perdita. The passage of time has ravaged her home but not she, for the lady is comely still. With hair as dark as a Raven's wing and eyes of cobalt blue, her beauty beguiles the starless night, for there is no other to gaze upon her countenance within these torn and empty walls. Softly, she sings a sad lament, fragments from a Troubadour's tale of a love long lost. Sorrow clouds her as a shroud. With downcast eyes and ethereal hands she takes soft strands of numinous threads and weaves silently through her tears. Through the telling of her silken tales there begins to unfold a story of love, a story of loss.

The lost love of a Knight of old. Her Knight...Her story...

To the soft strains of a melancholy Mandolin every stitch of the Knight's chivalrous deeds begin to unfold upon her fragile tapestry.

Sir Allard, encased in his suit of armour and clutching his sword of steel, mounted his dashing destrier. He basked in the admiration he drew from the assembly of illustrious Lords and Ladies, all too aware all eyes were on him. He smiled knowing both damsels and Dowagers were dazzled by his presence. As he graciously bestowed generous glances upon the Ladies fair, Perdita smiled trustingly. She knew within his brave breast beat the chivalrous heart of one who only had eyes for her. And so with a righteous fire burning in his heart and mounting his noble steed the valiant Knight bade Adieu to his assembled Court and proudly rode to war.

Satisfied with the vibrancy of the first scene, Perdita left her loom and her labour of love. Gazing out of the window her searching heart went forth once more into the blanket of night, looking and longing for her Gallant Knight who had sailed from England's green and pleasant lands to faraway shores. With a sigh she returned to her tapestry, intent on weaving the threads of her fragrant memories, did she know how their story would unfold?

There is a chill that pervades her bower, yet her shivers are not from cold, but the delightful anticipation of her noble Knight's triumphant return. The glory! The honour! How her heart sang joyfully for him! She wrapped her self in the warm glow of the sweet words of eternal love he had spoken. How her heart ached when she recalled her initial reluctance upset him so. His entreaties were urgent. Why would she not acquiesce to his burning desires? He protested his Lady was so cruel to tarry, for he had great perils to face. The sweet memories of her succour would comfort him upon the bloody battlefields. Surely his heart would rend in two if she did not return his love! Perdita was torn. She cried bitter tears. As a highborn Lady she would bring dishonour to her family if she lay with him without the sanctity of a wedding band. Kissing her tears away, her chivalrous Knight declared they would marry upon his victorious return from the beast of war. With lyrical persuasion Allard's conquest was assured. Cautioning Perdita to keep her own counsel and keep their tryst secret, he gave her a ring of gold set with a ruby. The dazzling red gemstone held the promise of eternal love and bought her silence.

Through the cloak of darkness a mote of light broke through the night, bringing momentary illumination. Perdita's fragile heart skipped a beat. Was that her Knight she saw? Cruel memories came crashing into her dreams. A tear fell. Her beloved had sailed away across the seven seas. He had abandoned his Lover to her fate and all for the King's glory, crusading in a faraway Land.

Watching the passage of many Moon tides from her lonely Bower she entreated the star clad night to light his way home, before her shame was there for all to see. Highborn Lady Perdita, who some may say was without blame, could not be seen to be robed in tarnished garments of dishonour as the seed of new life grew within her belly. Yet she held her head high, comforted by their unborn child's quickening and Allard's reassurances. For her Knight would surely return and she would be his wife, and all judgement would pass, would it not?

The dying embers of the old year brought tidings of great sorrow. Sir Allard would nevermore see the sunrise or set upon England's Sceptered Isle. Nor give his child his rightful name. Enemy and Gallantry had brought him to his knees. Ever true to her Love, Perdita kept her counsel well. For the Templar's cause her brave Knight willingly gave his life. For her family honour, Perdita gave hers.

They found her at the break of day, her lifeless and broken body lying at the foot of castle walls. A ruby ring upon her unwed hand glinted in the pale winter sunlight. The fallen Lady was laid to rest beneath her lonely bower whilst far away under an Eastern Sun her Lover sleeps beneath shifting sands.

The solitary passage of time has shrouded the castle walls in creeping ivy, shadows and gloom. Yet awaiting her Lover's return Perdita's ghost still sits by her loom, lingering midst the rot and decay, trusting Love eternal will raise their hearts from the ashes and dust of betrayal. Her Love lives on, though they are all long dead...Perchance, your steps take you through the ruined walls of the Castle Keep, they do say by pale moon light and night's embrace, you may yet hear the strains of a mandolin as the lonely Lady weeps within her ghostly bower.

Deep within the darkest heart of night
dance slender beams of soft Moon Light.

9 BEGUILED BY BEAUTY

Do you believe in love at first sight? If you had asked me that question six months ago I would have said categorically no. I am rational man with a rational job. That is until the day she crossed my path. I guess I was in the space to let her in. Life was getting mundane. You know yourself. You wake up, kiss the wife, go to work, come home, kiss the wife. Sleep.

Dreamless nights that pass too fast, then you wake up and do it all again. It's what we do. Without question. The days of wine and roses, who needs them? Once the golden band is on her finger, then the deal is sealed. Job done. Then time, crafty, insidious time, starts eating away at you. The minutes turn into years and you don't notice because you are so busy waking up, kissing the wife, going to work, coming home, kissing the wife and sleeping. Then somehow, without even knowing how it happens you don't kiss anymore. When did romance die? Where did you loose yourself? Then all you have is this familiarity and distance and a strange feeling that something is missing. A longing. A longing for what? How can you even answer the question when you know something is wrong, but you are scared of the answer? Too close a look and the careful world you have constructed to keep the wolf from the door and the bear firmly outside your cave is suddenly not so safe anymore. So the indefinable something 'wrong' becomes the new normal. And everything goes on the same, evenings spent alone downstairs, my wife upstairs with some pulp fiction for company. Vague stirrings of guilt. Why did she need to read that stuff? Didn't she have me? Vague stirrings of regret, we were all right weren't we? What if the romantic fix she got from the pages of her books didn't cut it and she wanted more, from me, or someone else? Would I have anything left to give, or even care? I thought about going up and joining her, taking the book out of her hand and telling I was here, I was real. Notice me. I wanted to tell her I had my own hopes, dreams and desires and if she would only listen then I would share them with her and she wouldn't be white noise anymore. But how do you come back from too many years of comfortably numb? I didn't want to look too closely at that and shoved the awkward feeling deep down inside and just let it go.

Time ticking away, your life ebbing, second by second. Every moment one-step closer to the grave and nothing in between. I had heard all about mid-life crisis, even knew a few of the boys at work who had gone through it. Hit forty and hit a brick wall. The sudden desire for a tattoo, a Harley, a fast car, even a quick fling or two with whoever was willing. I've seen it end in tears, broken hearts and broken bones. Not me, I thought, won't happen to me. No one told me about mid-life madness. No one told me about Love, not love like this. Obsessive, crazy, can't get her out of my mind love. I work, she's there. I drive, she's there. I'm sat across the table from my wife. We eat. We have nothing to say, apart from the usual catch up on the day stuff. It doesn't matter, because she is there. Inside my mind. My wife is talking, but long ago I ceased listening. White noise. I smile. I nod. I agree. Whatever she wants, whatever it takes. Eventually my tactics pay off and there is blessed peace. I indicate I will be up in a while and she goes to bed, alone. Silence washes over me, a soothing mantle. And all I want is to go off, alone too. I want to picture *her*, be with her, the woman living in my mind. But it's all a crazy dream. Or is it?

I first met her late one Friday night after a very long day in Manhattan's Financial District. I wanted to relax and the old fashioned comfort of Harry's Bar Midtown hit the right note. I should have asked the cab to take me home to Brooklyn Heights, instead I walked in off the busy street into a cavernous basement. The walls were lined with vintage photographs from Hollywood's golden days. The décor was oak and leather, low lights, discreet booths and reminiscent of a gentleman's club from a bygone age. Somewhere someone was playing smooth jazz on a saxophone. The bluesy notes washed over me, soothing, with the music literally hitting just the right note. Cigarette in one hand, single malt over ice in the other, I settled back into the comfort of a big leather chair. I took a deep drag of my nicotine hit. Through the haze of smoke she appeared. Long, long dark hair, falling in tumbling waves over her slender back. And her eyes. Oh those eyes. Luminous, lovely and inviting. She was a goddess and she was there, right in front of me. I sat up and paid more attention to a woman than I had in the last seven years. More attention than I had paid to my wife in the longest time. Did I feel guilty? No. There was something in me that needed her. And here she was, in all her radiant beauty and she was present, right here, right now, a timeless goddess of the silver screen invading the recesses of my hungry mind.

"The words you don't say speak louder than those you do." She was a mind reader as well. I covered my embarrassment with a slug of whiskey. I resisted the urge to ask her if she came here often. Despite her soft southern drawl it was obvious she was always here. I wondered just how many men had sat here and gazed on her loveliness. How many men had she looked at with those faraway eyes? How many men had thought of running their hands through her luxurious long locks, pulling her into a tight embrace and kissing those luscious lips. I was getting out of my depth. Stubbing out my cigarette and draining my drink I stood up to leave. At that moment I was lost and she knew it, catching my eye her gaze said, "You'll be back." And I was. I was finding reasons to go to Harry's bar with the boys or alone. Never with my wife. I knew Maude would be there. Waiting. That seductive gaze, those eyes, I could drown in the depths of emotional intensity. My wife truly would not have understood. How would I find the words to explain just how or why another woman's beauty had the power to speak to my very soul? Maude listened to me. I found myself pouring out how I felt about my wife, about myself. I told her I didn't understand just how we had ended up in this big freeze. Where was the passion, the magic? When had the fire gone out? I told Maude everything I could not tell my wife. I got the feeling she would have liked to meet my elusive wife. But how could I introduce them? How could I explain Maude, who she was and what she meant to me? I loved her for her beauty, her glamour and mystery. She had the allure of an icon of the silver screen. She was there, she was present but she wasn't. I could look but I could not touch. She had made that clear. But I could dream. You are innocent when you dream. Maude knew these things and she knew I adored her. She didn't judge me. There was no blame, no weight of disappointment for things I had done, and things I had failed to do. With Maude I was free to be me. A man with hopes fears and desires and she understood and that was huge, and with all my heart I wished my wife would too. I was out of my depth and I was drowning. I guess it was only a matter of time before my wife found out.

The questions had started. 'What time will you be home? Why are you late? Where have you been? Out with the boys *again*, really!' I had no answers. No excuses. I closed down. Maude or my wife? It was becoming a very hard call. Maude was becoming my drug of choice. I needed her. I didn't need the third degree. After all I was innocent, wasn't I? *Innocent when you dream*...And dream I did. As I climbed into bed each night I envisaged she was there with me accompanying me into the realms of fantasy.

'I am an actress,' she said, 'A weaver of dreams and a maker of magic!'

'Maude, you are luminous! Do you have a gold star on Hollywood Boulevard? Take me there!'

'My star is a long way from Hollywood. Search the night sky for the Morning star and you will find me. I am your Immortal Flame. I am your goddess of love. Always remember Love conquers all.'

Together we travelled the World and danced under starlight skies. We banqueted within Castle walls, she was my Princess and I her Knight and somewhere a Troubadour strummed a mandolin and sang of our love. We visited the Alhambra Palace, walked hand through the Court of the myrtles and beneath the Andalucía sun she whispered sweet words to me. In the shadow of the iconic monument to love, The Taj Mahal, I became her Rajah and whispered words of devotion to her, my beloved Rani.

The mornings came, I awoke next to my wife, with her back turned to me. The gulf between us was now an aching chasm and felt I a wrenching loss in the pit of my stomach.

The night they finally came face to face with each other is etched on my mind. A cold November and the big freeze between my wife and I was now arctic in its intensity. Something would have to give. Even a row would show there was some passion left, some depth of feeling. I felt so surplus to requirement, the weight of her disappointment in me was becoming a burden too heavy to handle.

'Don't wait up. I have to work very late. I may sleep at the office.' And I was out the door before she could question me. I had plans for tonight and I would face the music in the morning. Right now there was a fire raging and if I didn't quench it, then I risked being subsumed in the heat of my own desire and aching need to be with Maude.

I got to the bar early, before the evening rush. I wanted to be at our table where I had first set eyes on Maude. The bartender, now familiar with my order, started pouring my favourite single malt Scotch, Glenmorangie, over ice. I settled back into the comfort of the deep leather chair and lit a cigarette. This is where it had begun. Maude was waiting for me, beautiful as ever. Every time I gazed at her I saw perfection and paradoxes, beauty both beguiling and innocent. I wanted to reach out and protect her. I wanted to hold her in my arms and tell her I would keep the wolf from the door and bad at bay. I looked into her eyes looking at me from a distant place and time, and saw her sadness and saw her soul. She was a star from a bygone age that shone so bright she still lit up my lonely night. But she wasn't real. She was a fantasy. No matter how much I longed to take her in my arms, to love her, Maude would never be mine for she belonged in the firmament above. From her gaze I saw she knew that I, as so many others before and after me, would always be hers. A captive of beauty. It was time to say goodbye. It was over.

'Go home,' Maude said, 'what you see in me, you first saw in her. What you feel for me, you first felt for her and you will again.'

The weight of loss was too much to bear. The double life I had been leading, the freezing cold at home that had caused ice to form over my heart had been melted by the passion I had felt for a woman who was not my wife. I had been beguiled by beauty,

Maude had touched my soul and I would never be the same again. A great wracking sob clawed its way out of my throat and I sat, head in my hands and I cried.

I felt her arms around me. Warm, loving and strong. She sat on the arm of the leather armchair and cradled me. Slowly she pulled my hands from my tear stained face and her soft mouth gently kissed my sorrow away. I looked into her eyes and saw the depth of love she felt for me and my heart began to beat fast. She was so beautiful, she was here beside me and she wanted me...I took her by the hand and asked her would she come home with me because I very much wanted to make love to her. She stood up and pulled me to her. I kissed her with a passion and intensity I had long forgotten and all the love and feeling inside me washed away the years. I was a man with hopes, feelings and desires and my wife understood, she always had and that was why she was here tonight.

'How did you know?'

'I know you,' she replied. 'I saw the way you looked at her photographs on the Internet, over and over. I watched you fall under her spell. How many men has she enchanted? You are not the first and you will not be the last. I wanted you to look at me that way, the way you did before we both forgot why we had been enchanted by each other.'

'And you forgive me?'

'Yes. Maude's beauty is her gift to the world. Beauty that speaks to the soul. She spoke to you and her silent words told a story of love, romance, hope and desire. And I heard.'

As we walked hand and hand out into the New York night air we turned and took a final look at Maude Fealy, an Edwardian beauty and movie star from a bygone age, as she watched over us from her home encased in a silver frame on the 'wall of fame' at Harry's Hollywood bar.

At that hour just before dawn wakes a sleepy world, as I lay entwined with my wife I happened to look out at the night sky. And there she was, true to her word. Venus, goddess of love. The morning star.

10 I KNEW THESE PEOPLE

"I knew these people...once...It was a long time ago..."

She looked like she needed to talk, some fragmented ghost of a memory rattling around the caverns of her mind seeking to find a voice. So I pulled up a chair and sat down beside her and prepared to listen. After all, it is what I do. Listen. I listen a lot. People tell me things, always have. Seems to come from nowhere, the torrent of words, the secrets and the shames. I never judge. That is for the Man above not me.

A waiter came over. Smartly dressed with slicked back black hair, just a hint of grey kissing his temples and a smile that reached his rich brown eyes. I noted he was deferential without being subservient, in a very European way. I liked him and resolved to leave him a good tip. I saw he liked her, a lot. Did she like him? It was difficult to tell. There was a story hiding behind his smile, but that would be for another time. Right now was her time. She had something to say and I had a strong intuition I needed to hear it.

I ordered a pot of English Breakfast Tea, toast and marmalade, "Make that for two, please," I glanced at her and she nodded her approval at him.

"Très bon," he rewarded us both with a smile, hiding just a soupçon of merriment. This man did not take life too seriously at all. He really was very handsome and as he walked away a delicious hint of citrus and spice lingered in the air.

"Mmm," I sniffed appreciatively "Do I detect patchouli and sandalwood?"

"Indeed you do. Top notes and base notes. Quite enticing, isn't it? Clive Christian 1872," she replied with authority and I wondered if she was the one who had gifted him a very fine bottle of cologne.

We sat in comfortable companionship in the beautiful glass roofed Courtyard. Soft pink stucco walls wrapped the restaurant with the elegance of a bygone age. She asked me if this was my first visit to the Wallace Collection. I smiled and told her I often came here to Hertford House and take yet another admiring stroll through the sumptuous rooms of the museum, admiring the works of fine art, especially paintings depicting angels. I told her my Mother had first brought me here as a little girl.

"Mummy are Angels just make believe or are they really real like the elves with their black patent shoes with big silver buckles and fairies with their gossamer wings in my big picture book?" I had made earnest enquiries.

"Indeed they are Evie," Mummy had replied, "Would you like to see the lovely paintings of the Angels in Hertford House? We shall look at suits of armour and you can see for yourself knights who protected princesses were very real too! We shall have tea and toast and yummy jam when we finish."

My Mother always had a special way of making the most magical things sound a natural part of everyday life. I missed her and gazing at my elegant companion momentarily wondered would Mummy have looked just like her if the sickness had not came and took her away much too soon. Would we be sitting here now recalling my delight at the moment I had gazed on the beautiful paintings of Lords and Ladies of long ago. Entranced by the many treasures housed in the Wallace Collection, I had moved from one sumptuous and ornate gallery to the next, each filled with armour, fine porcelain, ornate snuffboxes and gorgeous fireplaces and rococo chandeliers. And I had seen the Angels. And I had believed.

I saw I was under close scrutiny, "I like it here," I told her, " I like it a lot. It's been a long love affair," I said.

She smiled and told me she loved it too, had been visiting the imposing Georgian house, standing proudly on London's Manchester Square, for as long as she could remember. She said that she loved the Gainsborough's and Fragonard's. She smiled in appreciation as she divulged her favourite painting and said she found Scheffer's "The Ghosts of Paolo and Francesca Appear to Dante and Virgil" hauntingly beautiful. She said it made her cry. She told me she hugely admired the serenity of Velázquez's black veiled beauty "The Lady with a Fan" and shared she was intrigued by sculptures depicting veiled beauties. She wondered if

Raffaele Monti's emotive statuette truly depicted a Circassian slave? Perhaps, she postulated, she was truly free and her beautiful veiled countenance was an allegory for her seeing 'beyond the veil' into numinous realms. She said her name was Evelyn and she had a town house close by in Crawford Street, she was a Writer and she was glad of my company. A lot of words as one would expect, but not what she really needed to say.

I shivered involuntarily. Crawford Street was a place I knew well, having grown up in an elegant stucco fronted Georgian house. In different circumstances I would be living there now, but for the premature loss of my darling Mother. That house held many happy memories and I had vowed one day to return, that it would be my home again. Meeting Evelyn was proving to be more than a touch synchronistic.

Our tea and toast arrived."Those people...?" I tried to engage her to take my mind away from wandering down dark avenues from the past.

I poured tea, fragrant with freshly pressed leaves, from a pewter pot into our cups and she added the milk and sugar. The toast was good. I ladled on rich yellow butter and a generous helping of deliciously bitter marmalade and as I savoured the flavours I waited for her to speak. You can have an intuition on what they may say, sometimes hear the words before they actually speak them. Then when they do speak, the emotions come in, sometimes softly flowing, sometimes a tidal wave. And I have it all hitting me, sometimes it's hard to remain inscrutable, to just listen. But it is about them, not me, so they never know I have eyes that look into their distant pasts and possible futures, their right here, right now's or just how much I know...

She was different. Looking at me quizzically with intelligent eyes, and with a start I realised she was reading me reading her. A feint smile. I winked at her, knowingly. We laughed conspiratorially.

Sunlight, delicately streaming through the glass roof caught her hair. Cool blonde with strands of silver pulled off her face by a black velvet band. A woman of a certain age, but what that age was I would be hard pressed to say. Quietly understated elegance. She wore pearl earrings. Beautiful pearls, soft as moonlight. I admired them.

"Indeed yes, they are beautiful. Tears from the moon." Her eyes misted. I reached over and covered her hand with mine. A simple gesture, speaks more eloquently and deeply than words ever can. She had long slim fingers tipped with manicured nails varnished the colour of her pale pink pearls. Her hand was surprisingly cold.

"Those people..." I encouraged, knowing the earrings held the key to her story, as did love. Was it lost, unrequited, had her heart been broken or did she carry the heavy weight of human frailty having inflicted pain and hurt on another? I munched my toast waiting for her to reply. The toast here is really very good. My reward for patience just a flicker behind her grey eyes, a wry smile and the deafening sound of silence. Perhaps a guilty conscience lay behind her insouciance? I truly hoped not.

Suddenly I had a very strong desire to know and held her gaze searchingly. I saw the relief in her face as the waiter returned with a fresh pot of tea and she took the opportunity to slip her hand away from mine, the shutters were down. The moment had passed. I got she was uncomfortable with my touch, the warmth of another human reaching out to her. I wasn't sure if she would tell me her story, or keep her secrets to be shared only with the ghost living in the caverns of her mind. With a start, I realised I could not read her, looking into her eyes all I saw was myself looking back, my pale pink pearls catching rainbows of light as the sun danced through the atrium.

She may well have a lifetime of stories to tell, but I was going to have to live them before Evelyn shared our secrets with me, Evie...

11 SCENES OF SEDUCTION

The enticing scent of Jasmine, Bergamot and Rose Absolute delighted Valentina's senses. She watched the steam rise, misting windows and mirrors. The frenetic energy of Mid-Town, New York on the busy streets below receded into an amorphous dreamscape as she sunk into a fragrant cocoon of bubbles and deliciously warm water. The deep bath, an oasis of peace for her tired mind to drift far away from the horror of the day. For a while. As she stepped out of the tub onto the biting cold black marble floor, unwelcome images came tearing like a vicious tornado into her mind. She bit her trembling lip and bid them go. There was no time for tears, she needed to hurry if she were to be ready for Alessandro. With steel resolve, she denied the howling thoughts a voice. Grabbing a fresh cotton bath sheet, she wrapped it as a comforting hug around her voluptuous body. Shaking her long midnight hair loose, she envisaged Alessandro's hands running through the silken strands. For the first time in hours, a smile played across her lips. With a shiver of delight, she felt his Presence drawing near. Valentina could almost sense him watching as she sat at her dressing table, preparing for him, just as he liked her. She was a natural beauty but a little Hollywood glamour always added a frisson of excitement. When she looked good, she felt good. Valentina reached for her cosmetics. Heavy mascara stroked over her long lashes, a sweep of smoky grey shadow and deep obsidian eyes outlined in black kohl. The smouldering, sultry look he adored. A kiss of Chanel Rouge Allure red lipstick and she was ready to meet the promise of the night ahead. Valentina liberally sprayed his favourite Italian perfume, Bottega Veneta, on all the places he would kiss, shivering in delicious anticipation of the delights of the night to come. Slipping into an elegant black velvet cocktail dress, she pulled the lush fabric over her delicate La Perla satin scarlet lingerie. Valentina intent on setting a scene of soft seduction, stretched out her long legs and slowly peeled up a pair of sheer stockings, edged with lace. She appraised herself in the mirror. Italian class and Fifth Avenue elegance. Almost perfect. All that was needed was a pair of impossibly high red stiletto heels. She stepped into her Christian Louboutin's with practiced ease. The soft glow of a myriad of candles lit the room, flickering flames reflected in gorgeous crystal glasses filled with fine imported French wine, a delicious vintage Claret. A decanter of

Brandy, Grey Goose Vodka and lines of white powder, rolled up $100 banknotes, and a silver tray peppered with a cocktail of pills. Time to party hard. It would be an intense night. The way they liked it.

The lady waited, looking out at the twinkling lights as the City below slipped into the heart of the night. She smiled thinking about all those shows on Broadway, she had a special performance of her own tonight in her luxurious penthouse hotel suite. In the background music played, an adagio by Pachelbel, low and slow. The scene has been set for an evening of soft seduction and a long night of unbridled passion.

He's late. She doesn't mind. They have time. An eternity of love awaits. A little drink and a line while she plays the waiting game. She isn't worried, he will show when he is ready, just as he always has done for the last seven years. A guy in his line of work gets caught up in things. She understands that. He knows, and loves her for it. No judgement. No blame. Loves him as he is, raw and real and all hers. Only hers, if she was free to be his too without recrimination and without sin. If only it was his ring she wore. Two hearts beating in two separate worlds. So near, so far. Upper East Side, Manhattan Socialite and Staten Island Wise Guy, connected by the Verrazano-Narrows Bridge, business, commerce and justice.

Another glass of blood red wine, another line of pure white Snow. Anticipating a discreet knock on the hotel room door. She intuitively knows it will be soon and changes the tempo of the music, Ravel's Bolero fits perfectly and she is ready to slide into his waiting arms and dance to the rhythm of love. Yet more wine, the last line. The red and blue pills have all gone. The hour is late, her Lover even later. Yet she does not fret, waits patiently, knowing he will come for her and so she takes sweet repose laid out upon the rich damask coverings on the King sized bed.

The Sanctum prided itself on being an oasis of discreet calm midst the hustle and bustle of Manhattan. Corey loved his job as Concierge at the boutique hotel. The building was an eclectic blend of quiet elegance and modern chic. It was one of Mid Town's best kept secrets. A place to restore and replenish without leaving New York City. Discretion was key and many a well- known face in need of a little time out had slipped quietly into its soothing walls.

Of course Corey knew who Valentina Venichi was. Her face graced the pages of the society magazines he loved so well. For seven years she had escaped the gilded cages of the Manhattan Townhouse and beach front Mansion in East Hampton and the life of a trophy wife. With her European pedigree, the penniless Contessa Valentina Venichi was no more than a classy accessory to her Ivy League husband, Judge McKensie Denton III, twenty years her senior. A wife in name only, her husband's tastes lay elsewhere. She had never truly fitted into the upper echelons of Manhattan socialite society. The Judge was both respected and feared. He was not known to be a kind man.

Valentina had Mediterranean blood in her veins, she was warm and vibrant and too many lonely nights in her lonely bed had led to stolen kisses in a smoky club and secret nights. Same time, same place, a yellow cab to Mid-Town to meet him, the Uptown girl and her downtown New Jersey guy. Escape from her reality and his too, the intimate boutique hotel, their suite, the glamour of illicit pleasures. The Concierge knew his tastes in fine wines and hers in Colombian lines and all would be waiting. Discretion assured. Always. Knew her name and his too, but never a whisper. Discretion being the name of the well paid game.

Corey had shown surprise at her unexpected appearance tonight. He had seen the news reels. She was dressed in a sombre black suit, carrying the New York Times late edition. Incongruous dark sunglasses on a grey Winter's night were hiding something, regret, grief, tears? But discreet as ever no questions were asked, her suite was made ready to the lady's tastes. A generous tip and Corey slipped away, making a mental note he would make sure to check on her before his shift ended, as he always had. Paramedics, an adrenalin shot and a precautionary visit to the nearest E.R only once in Seven years were a testament to his vigilance and care. The man who loved her had rewarded his loyalty many times, yet Corey had genuinely grown very fond of the Lady. Knew her challenges, and where his own sympathies lay.

Dawn broke brittle and sharp over the grey New York skyline. The candles long burnt out and Valentina's elegant Italian scent replaced by the repugnant smell of excess. Empty bottles strewn across the floor, dregs of the rich blood red wine clinging to the sides of one crystal glass, the other filled to the brim, untouched stood in lonely isolation next to a crumpled $100 bill, liberally coated in cocaine. The Concierge knocked once for decency and entered.

Corey picked up her discarded clothing, reverently clearing the debris and detritus of distress. The black lace stockings, the gorgeous Louboutin shoes, lingerie and Ballenciaga designer dress all went into the trash too. She'd always been an Uptown girl, classy dame, an Italian Princess. With a forensic eye he cleaned the scene. Hung up her sharp suit and shirt, placed the elegant black leather pumps and quietly elegant Chanel bag in the wardrobe too.

Yesterday's newspaper, lay tossed on the floor, he folded it with care into the almost full trash bag. His eyes misted at the front page photo of an extremely handsome man, Italian descent, tanned with dancing cobalt blue eyes and dressed in a sharp Armani suit. For a moment in time, his dazzling smile was caught on camera as he confidently walked into New York's imposing Central Court

House to face trial for racketeering under the RICO Statute. In the background, the stern face of the District Attorney, Vittore DiAngelo stared smugly at the baying press pack. They scented blood and he was the man to deliver the kill as the Judge, McKensie Denton III prepared in his chambers as his loyal wife stood on the court room steps watching the spectacle of the most high profile case of her illustrious husband's career unfold.

Rumoured to have been gunned down by a rival crime family, Alessandro Bianchi would no longer face a Federal Court nor would he succeed his powerful Father to head the most powerful crime family in New York. A sniper's bullet had shattered both those dreams and his cranium into a starburst of bone and blood on the cold stone stairs of the illustrious courthouse. Valentina had gently kissed his image with her Rouge Allure red lips and smudged the copy with her bitter tears. Allowing a wave of emotion to ride over him, and with respect, Corey covered her naked body with a fresh silk sheet before dialling 911 for help with an unresponsive and unknown guest. Discretion, as always, assured. Even in death.

At the breaking of a brand new day, dawn had rose above the New York skyline. Soft rain cleansing the streets below. When her Lover finally made his appearance, Valentina was ready. She saw him approaching through a diaphanous haze. As handsome in death as in life. "I knew you would keep your promise and never leave me, Ti Amo, Alessandro." With a seductive smile, dark eyes blazing Alessandro approached and took his Valentina in his arms. Soft music played, bodies swayed. The gift of one last dance before they fell into love's eternal embrace. Valentina had chosen an eternity with Alessandro rather than a lifetime of regret with the upstanding Judge McKensie Denton III, her proud and vengeful husband. Who had refused to let her go when she had asked for a divorce to marry the man she truly loved. The weight of his wealth and family name was not enough to keep her shackled. McKenzie had shown no mercy. He had aspirations to the Supreme Court. He'd be damned if they were dashed by his disgrace of a wife taking up with a Mobster. Under the guise of impartially presiding over the trial of Alessandro Bianchi , he had callously sentenced him to death by whispering in the ear of a well- connected Senator at one of his high power soirées at The Hamptons mansion. Men in high places would tumble and fall if Bianchi were to take the Stand. Far better if he were to fall instead? The tame and corrupt District Attorney Vittore DiAngelo had been given a nod and it had been set in motion. The sentence had been passed before the trial had even began. The day Alessandro had walked up the stone steps into his courthouse, The Judge had ensured Valentina was waiting beside the callous D.A, along with the assembled press pack. An unknown assassin's bullet had ripped through the air and her Lover had fallen dead. His red blood a stain on justice. They were both now far beyond the confines of her vindictive husband and *his* law...

12 OVER THE SEA TO SKYE

"Wild is the beauty Of Barra's Land
Harsh Waves Crash Upon Silver Sand
My True Love Abandoned Me Today
Left Our Unborn Child To Sail Away
Brought To My Knees, Left in Poverty
For A siren's Call Across The Seven
Seas"

I've always been fascinated by abandoned places and the fragments of the past lingering in the stale air. Is it the remnants of lost hopes, I sense? Fragments of dreams and burnt out desires? The Croft was one of those places with so many stories to tell and I wanted to hear them.

Tapping into residual energies? It is what I do, never questioned it, accepting it just 'is what it is.' They never leave, those old ghosts from the past, their memories becoming just another layer on the atmosphere. And if they chose to reveal their secrets, as a whisper on the wind, then I have a greedy ear to listen.

I walked over to a small wooden framed window, dirty panes of glass, eyes dully staring without seeing, the wild beauty of the land. The taste of sea salt hung in the air flung up by harsh waves beating down upon soft silver sands. Who stood there, looking out at me looking in? Did they ever wonder what lay on the edge of the horizon, what lay over the sea from Barra to Skye. Intrigued and wanting to know more I approached the door, coated in peeling paint of soft pink and covered in lichen.

It beckoned to be opened. I reached out and grasped the iron handle, blackened and rusted with age, expecting it to be cold to the touch. Instead I felt it crackle as a jolt of electricity ran up my arm. The magic had begun, hands from the past were still imprinted on the handle. A melancholy creak and the door opened, allowing me admittance to a forgotten world. Who would be waiting and would they be willing to speak? Would I have too many questions, for which there were too few answers?

And then I heard her! A soft whisper in my ear as gentle as the kiss of a summer breeze.

"I'm still here."

"Talk to me," I said, "tell me your story." And she did.

Flora was her name, a bonny lass with red hair, flowing like molten lava down her slim back. She shyly lifted her head to look at me, her eyes filled with innocent guise, and matching her simple muslin dress, a splash of cobalt blue in a grey place.

The impressions came flooding in, gossamer threads of the fabric of her life. She'd loved him and leaving the comfort and protection of her Father's castle walls ran away with her Sailor boy, freely crossing over the sea from Skye to be with him in the croft.

Life was harsh but Flora comforted herself when it was cold outside the flames of passion and desire he ignited in her were all she needed. The warmth of his love and the fire burning brightly in the grate would keep bad at bay. Until the fire went out, leaving ashes and dust...

Slowly Flora came to realise she was not enough for her man. She shared him with his Mistress. It was a bitter blow to see his eyes light up when he heard the siren's call, in a way they no longer did for her. With sad resignation Flora knew, once his Mistress summoned him, he would go. Much as he loved his young wife, when the sea whispered his name, he was lost.

Many a moon tide she stood waiting upon a lonely shore, looking out to sea and praying for his safe return. He would return. He always did once the yearning to be free and sail the seven seas had been assuaged, then he would hold her and love her and she would forgive and forget. Hope burnt brightly within her innocent heart. He was her lover, her friend and husband in the eyes of God above and father of her children yet to be born. Bonny bairns who would play at her feet. Strong sons who one day would go to sea and ease their poverty, such dreams had she!

I sensed the atmosphere change. Anticipation, excitement and the thrill of laying in his arms replaced by a dull dread.

Silence. She was fading.

"What happened, can you tell me?"

Outside the sky was blackening, dark storm clouds approached. I smelt the promise of rain, harsh and bitter.

"Ohh...Flora..." I felt her pain, "Talk to me..." I heard the rasp of the door swinging open. She had no words left. It was time to go. I took a final look around and followed her out. The croft was empty, love did not live here anymore.

The tide was going out and I made haste down to the beach, passing a rocky outcrop of granite monoliths. Had she too passed this way? Were the stones silent sentinels witnessing her silent scream as day became night and night day as she waited, fear descending as a clammy shroud. At the closing of the day, as the light was fading away, I saw her standing there upon her lonely shore. Calling, calling...

But her love did not hear, for he was lost to the deep embrace of a cold, cruel sea. The siren had called. He would not return. Her words were carried on the wind over the sea to Skye for no one to hear but me...

NIGHTSHADES

BOOKS BY EILY NASH

Paranormal Fiction

Torn From The Heart
Wychwood

Short Stories

Gossamer Threads
Nightshades
Meet Me At Midnight

Chick Lit with Angel Nash

Angelicious!
Telling Tails
Angel In The City
Angel Cake

Books for children with Ryan Nash

Magdalena
Poppy Paws & Patch
Puppy Paws

Poetry

Hymn To Her
Obsidian Eyes
Noir Nocte

WYCHWOOD

Dr Lucis Ferre is a dashing, debonair heart surgeon, the man of fragile Ellis Harwood's dreams. Falling under his spell, she soon realizes things are not as they seem. Lucis has a heart of darkness, forged in the foundry of his secret occult practices. On a harrowing winter's night, Ellis' life is hanging by a thread, as the dream brutally becomes a nightmare.

Does Ellis have an Angel waiting in the wings to offer deliverance from the evil doctor and sanctuary from his cruelty?

By a twist of fate, Ellis finds herself in the Hamlet of Wychwood. It is a place where the veil between worlds is gossamer thin, nothing is quite as it seems and magic abounds. Enigmatic Peter Cabot, local country Doctor and Hepzibah, his eccentric housekeeper, set about healing her battered body and bruised heart. But the malevolent Lucis has unfinished business.

Will Wychwood weave its magic spell, or will Ellis choose to go back to her evil husband.... A choice must be made.....

ISBN-10: 147016440X
ISBN-13: 978-1470164409

TORN FROM THE HEART

Adam Knight is a heartbreaker. With his boyish charm and good looks, he is used to women falling at his feet. Stunned to wake and find his young wife, Callie, has left him in the dead of night taking baby Tyler with her. He abandons plans for another illicit tryst with his amoral secretary and takes off to the countryside without the lascivious Sherrie in tow. Can Adam come up with a strategy to win Callie back and continue with his bad boy ways?

Walking on the open Moors of the Somerset Levels, a wild storm springs out of nowhere, catching Adam unawares. Lashed by the unrelenting elements, he falls and injures himself. With night rapidly riding in and no help at hand, he is in very real danger. Alone and afraid he cries out for help....in the middle of nowhere, will anyone hear his plea?

His prayers are answered, as he stumbles upon the decrepit and ancient 'Half Moon Inn'. It is a world apart from the luxurious Country House Hotel he is staying. Adam's luck seems to change when Inn Keeper Evelyn Blackmore offers sanctuary and offers the hurt, hungry, and frightened man refuge. As they prepare to spend the hours of darkness alone together, the wild storm continues to rage outside. Evelyn weaves magical fireside tales to while away the hours until the stranded stranger can cross the Moor in safety back to his hotel

However, the beautiful and fey woman is not all she seems to be. Adam finds she has a way of eliciting his inner most secrets. Forced to confront his own heart of darkness will he forget his marital woes and continue with his plans to seduce the beguiling Evelyn? Or have his past sins caught up with him? As the night progresses, the reasons behind his cruel womanising ways are torn from the recesses of his heart. Evelyn offers Adam the gift of healing more than his injured body, but will he reach out to her and accept? Moreover, if he does, is she able to cure the hole in his soul, or will she too be seduced into his dark web of deceit? The tables are unexpectedly turned on Adam, as he starts to fall under Evelyn's bewitching spell. She is unlike any woman he has been attracted to before; fragile and beautiful with her delicate features, raven eyes and flowing black hair. There is definitely something mysterious and different about Evelyn Blackmore and her witch like ways. Could there be a touch of magic in the air?

ISBN-10: 1470164353
ISBN-13: 978-1470164355

Thank you for reading.

www.edendenebooks.com

Printed in Great Britain
by Amazon

29816669R00071